Gosh look Teddy, it's a Werewolf

Bob Wilson

Collins

Look out for more *Jumbo Jets* from Collins

First published by A & C Black Ltd in 1996
Published by Collins in 1996

Collins is an imprint of HarperCollins*Publishers*Ltd,
77–85 Fulham Palace Road, Hammersmith, London W6 8JB

ISBN 978-0-00-675173-1

Text and illustrations © Bob Wilson 1996

The author/illustrator asserts the moral right to
be identified as the author and the illustrator of the work.
A CIP record for this title is available from the British Library.

CHAPTER ONE
The Hideous Secret!!

The story begins with

SNOBBERLY HOUSE

A Highly Esteemed
Academic Establishment

Dedicated to the
enlightenment & refinement
of genteel young ladies

PROSPECTUS
1996-7

In other words—
A POSH GIRLS' SCHOOL.

If you were to read the school prospectus
you would be told that the school was . . .

Graciously situated
in its own grounds in a building largely
unaltered since the time of
George the Third

In these idyllic surroundings girls are taught
the traditional subjects using
well-tested, time-honoured methods.

THE ACADEMIC STAFF

The Academic Staff are all highly qualified
Educationalists with many years of extensive
pedagogical experience behind them.

You would also be told
that the school had . . .

A NOBLE TRADITION

Snobberly House girls are expected to take
Pride in the school and its uniform,
and to conduct themselves with
Grace and dignity at all times.

Snobberly House encourages girls to develop
A spirit of fortitude and self-reliance.

Above all we like to think that
Snobberly House is
A HAPPY SCHOOL

Finally you would see a photograph of a group of fifth-formers enjoying a *'really exciting'* Geography lesson – and you would be told . . .

BUT <u>what you wouldn't be told</u> was that behind the posh, smiling facade of Snobberly House School there lurked

A
HiDEOUS
SECRET!

CHAPTER TWO
Sweet Primrose

Primrose Hill was by nature a kind . . .

EXCUSE ME?

Who's that?

Me. The person that's reading this story.

Oh, hullo. What d'you want?

Aren't you going to tell us about this HIDEOUS SECRET?

No. Not just yet.

Why not!?

It's not the right time. You'll get to find out about the Hideous Secret soon enough.

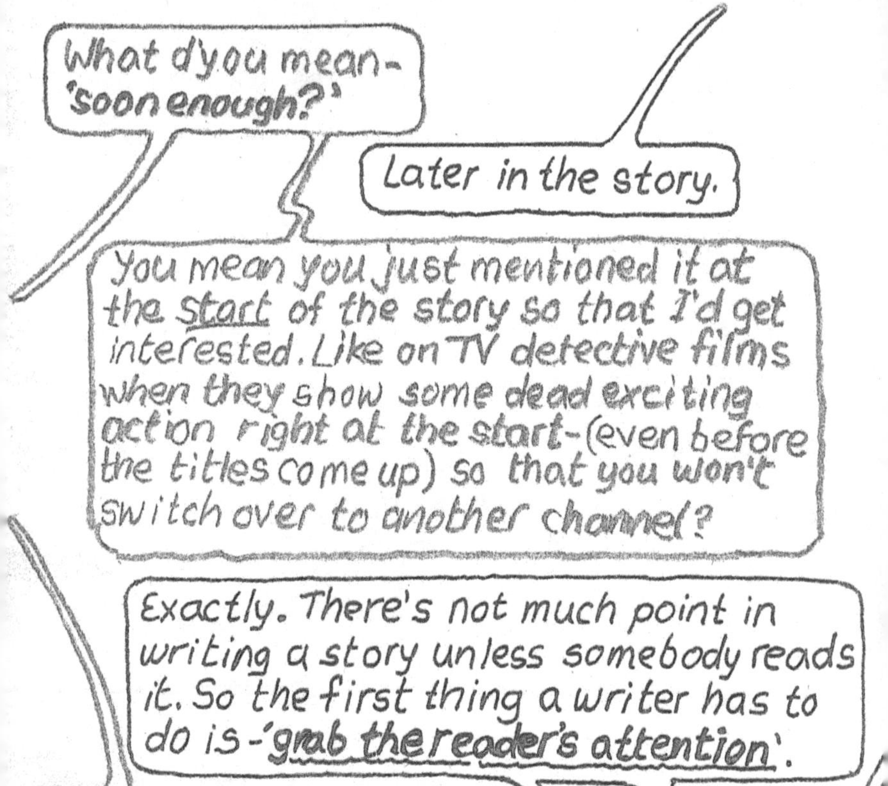
What d'you mean- 'soon enough?'
Later in the story.
You mean you just mentioned it at the start of the story so that I'd get interested. Like on TV detective films when they show some dead exciting action right at the start-(even before the titles come up) so that you won't switch over to another channel?
Exactly. There's not much point in writing a story unless somebody reads it. So the first thing a writer has to do is-'grab the reader's attention'.
Okay. So you've got my attention. Now what?
I'm going to try to introduce the main elements of the plot in such a way as to arouse the reader's curiosity and create dramatic tension.
Crikey! What does that mean!?
Exactly. You'll have to.. wait and see.

Primrose loved flowers and birds.

Indeed she loved <u>the whole of nature</u>
(especially the environment).
She also worried about it a lot.

(Especially the hole in the ozone layer.)

But on the particular night which begins this part of the story, Primrose was worried by something even more alarming than the thought that greenhouses might start falling through holes in the ozone layer. A vital part of her world was in terrible danger and only <u>she</u> could avert the looming catastrophe. She worked on the problem late into the night.

She had got to discover – by <u>tomorrow morning</u> – the scientific reason why the increased levels of carbon dioxide in the atmosphere, produced by the burning of fossil fuels, was causing the Sahara Desert to grow at a rate of forty-seven thousand square miles per year . . .

OR ELSE! ➔

... Brenda Pigg would rip the head off her Teddy Bear.

Brenda Pigg.

'CUDDLES'

A NOTE FROM THE AUTHOR Now, you may think that Primrose was worrying unnecessarily.

But you don't know Brenda Pigg!

If you knew Brenda Pigg and she'd threatened to rip the head off your Teddy if you didn't do her Geography homework for her — you'd believe that she would actually do it if you didn't.

In fact if you knew Brenda Pigg, and she said so, you'd probably be prepared to believe that if you didn't do her Geography homework she'd go to South America, destroy a rain forest, build greenhouses all over it, and then rip the head off your teddy JUST FOR FUN!

You mean she was a bully?

Correct!

CHAPTER THREE
A rude awakening

At last the problem was solved and
Primrose got to bed. She slept peacefully
that night believing that Cuddles was safe.
But next morning, when she gave the
homework essay to Brenda Pigg, Brenda
didn't say thank you.
She said –

I don't know what you see in that stupid bear anyway. It's a stupid baby thing. I've a good mind to rip its head off anyway. **Give it here!**

And who knows what might
have happened had someone
not shouted –

Brenda Pigg. STOP THAT AT ONCE!

It was Miss Fitt, their form teacher.
At first Primrose was greatly relieved,
but then she was absolutely horrified
because Miss Fitt then said –

And she marched off down the corridor
with Cuddles clasped under her arm.

said Brenda Pigg.

CHAPTER FOUR
An odd occurrence

Miss Fitt put Cuddles on her desk and Primrose was forbidden to touch; she could only stare and think – and the thought of him being left alone in an empty school for a whole weekend was quite unbearable.

When home-time came that night she waited in the corridor until everyone had gone. Then she crept back into the classroom. She thought perhaps she could . . . **But he wasn't there!**

Now you might think it odd that a teacher should take a teddy bear home with her for the weekend – but you don't know Miss Fitt.
Miss Fitt had a reputation amongst the girls for being **extremely odd**.

CHAPTER FIVE
The extreme oddness of Miss Jennifer Fitt

There were a number of things about Miss Fitt that struck the girls in her class as being rather odd.

For example:

1 Once she'd dropped her handbag in the playground and some unusual things had fallen out.

Bicycle clips.

She always came to school on the Bus.

A tin of dog food

she didn't have a dog.

A pair of dark, sunglasses.

It was December →

And a razor.

←!? she had the hairiest legs in school.

2 Once Melanie Penge just happened to mention that her brother was a wolf cub and that he'd just got his homecraft badge . . . and Miss Fitt had screeched

3 Every day, as soon as the bell went, Miss Fitt grabbed her coat, shouted '**The darkness is coming!**', and ran out of the classroom. Other teachers didn't do this. They stayed behind to organise after-school activities. There were many activities Miss Fitt could have joined in with – but didn't. For instance:

On Mondays there was choir practice.
On Tuesdays there was cycling proficiency.
On Wednesdays there was netball training.
On Thursdays the drama group rehearsed
for the Christmas pantomime.
And on one particular Friday after the school secretary had first tried to do the timetables on the new computer

19

the fourth form choir dressed up as
the seven dwarfs, and bicycled their way
into the semi-finals of the inter-schools,
County Netball Championship.

④

Only once had Miss Fitt ever been seen out
after dark.

Cynthia Scott-Bimbo claimed that late one
night, looking through her bedroom
window, she'd seen somebody, who <u>she
thought</u> might have been Miss Fitt, cycling
up Hill Street towards the edge of town,
with a paper bag on her head.

'How could you see if it was so late at night, anyway?' sneered Brenda Pigg.

There was a full moon,

replied Cynthia.

21

CHAPTER SIX
The question was – Why?

In truth, none of the girls really knew why Miss Fitt behaved so strangely. But they each had their own theory.

Primrose said –

Maybe she's a member of a secret society - like the Freemasons. They wear peculiar things.

Mistress Fitt. Thou art now a member of the Ancient Baghead Club.

More likely she's a spy for the Dutch Secret Police. They ride bicycles.

said Melanie.

Cynthia was inclined to think that Miss Fitt was having a secret love affair with an under-age barber, or some working-class person who lived in a pet shop.

'Rubbish,' said Brenda Pigg.

It's obvious that she's a mad, spell-casting witch who spends her evenings torturing Teddy Bears and turning wimpy schoolgirls into frogs!

Tin of dog food, eye of newt...

Preposterous though these theories were, they were more credible than the truth. **Because, you see, the truth was**

CHAPTER SEVEN
A change for the worse

Primrose had to spend a . . .

EXCUSE ME?

Yes, what now?

Has 'THE UNBELIEVABLY AWFUL TRUTH' got anything to do with 'THE HIDEOUS SECRET'?

You'll have to wait and see.

Is this what's called – 'keeping the reader in suspense'?

Yes.

But when will...

Listen. This book's got to be exactly 64 pages long. If I keep using up space in order to answer your questions we'll have got to the end of the book before we've got to the end of the story – and then you'll never know the 'AWFUL TRUTH.'

Oh...right. Sorry. You carry on then.

Back to the story ➤

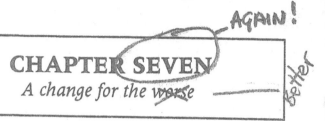

CHAPTER SEVEN
A change for the worse

AGAIN!

Better

Primrose had to spend a whole weekend without Cuddles and by Monday morning she was not just lonely, miserable and sad, **she was ferociously irritable.**

But Miss Fitt was in a strangely pleasant mood. At the start of the lesson she gently placed Cuddles on top of the book cupboard, and said –

Each evening Miss Fitt took Cuddles home with her and each morning she arrived at school in an even better mood.

On Tuesday morning she told a joke.

On Wednesday she let her hair down.

On Thursday she hung about after school chatting with the caretaker.

And on Friday she announced –

Miss Fitt said that the casual winter visitor might think that the bare, bleak hills of the Derbyshire Peak District were lonely and boring. But in fact they *teemed with interesting nature* and were full of *vitality, warmth, humour and life.*

She'd been reading a book about it.

At the end of the day Primrose asked Miss Fitt if she could have Cuddles back now. Miss Fitt said, 'But of course you may', and smiled warmly. **But afterwards . . .**

'The Derbyshire Peak District,' Miss Fitt
had said. 'What sort of things do you hope
to find there? Think about this over the
weekend and write me a list.'
Primrose knew what she hoped to see;
she didn't have to think about it.

Nor did Brenda.

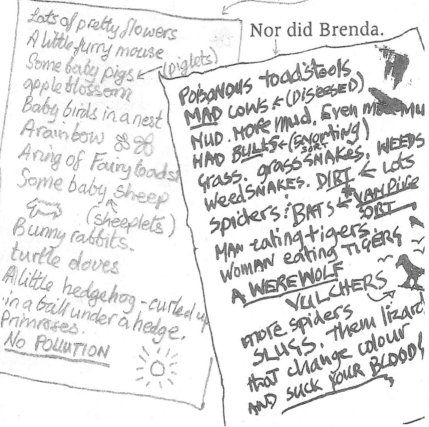

Lots of pretty flowers
A little furry mouse
Some baby pigs ← (piglets)
apple blossom
Baby birds in a nest
A rainbow
A ring of Fairy toads
Some baby sheep
(sheeplets)
Bunny rabbits.
turtle doves
A little hedgehog – curled up
in a ball under a hedge.
Primroses.
No POLLUTION

POISONOUS toadstools
MAD cows ← (DISEASED)
MUD. MORE MUD. EVEN MORE MUD
MAD BULLS ← (SNORTING SORT)
Grass. grassSNAKES. WEEDS
WEEDSNAKES. DIRT ← LOTS
spiders! BATS ← VAMPIRE SORT
DIRT
MAN eating tigers
WOMAN eating TIGERS
A WEREWOLF
VULCHERS
MORE spiders
SLUGS. Them lizard
that change colour
AND SUCK YOUR BLOOD!

But Cynthia did.
Cynthia gave the problem a lot of thought.

Finally she began her list.
She typed ➜ A districkt
    Followed by ➜ in Derbyshire
Then, struck by a sudden flash of
inspiration, she added

CHAPTER NINE
Introducing Everard Slogg

Everard Slogg was a farmer.

MUDGUSSET FARM

And, as chance would have it, he lived in
the Derbyshire Peak District.

Everard was at home in the bleak, bare
hills, and he was quite interested in the
interesting nature.

But, unlike Janet and John Wellbeloved,
his life was not filled with vitality, warmth,
and humour. *It was full of emptiness.*

Everard Slogg was a lonely bachelor.

He'd had a girlfriend once – years ago.
They met at the young farmers' dance.
Her name was Jennifer.

It was a clear case of love at first sight.

They went out walking together late into the evening, and had secret cuddles, and long, interesting conversations.

They found solace in each other's company.

I'd probably be on a rampage up in the hills; biting the heads off a flock of sheep.

How often in the voyage of love, has the ship of hope foundered on the rocks of a simple, unguarded reply such as this.
And so it was with Everard and Jennifer; they never saw each other again.

And often now, as Everard Slogg trudged wearily back to his lonely farmhouse after a long, hard day, he wished there was a friendly face waiting by the stove to greet him. But the house was always empty.
He had no wife, no friends – and visitors rarely came to Mudgusset Farm.

CHAPTER TEN
The oddness of Everard

Every day Farmer Slogg rose at dawn and worked until dusk out in the fields – dry stone walling, muck spreading, digging ditches. The work was hard and relentless. Most evenings after supper he'd be too tired to do much. Usually he'd have a shave, perhaps watch TV for an hour or so, then beginning to feel a bit sleepy, he'd stretch, yawn, feed the dog, wind up the clock – and turn in to bed.

You probably think that Everard Slogg was a typical Derbyshire hill farmer.

But you'd be wrong.

Because **some evenings**, usually after a dreary day and almost certainly if it was a full moon night, he wouldn't bother to have a shave or turn on the TV. Instead he'd just sit, watching the hairs grow on the back of his hands. Then, beginning to feel a bit creepy, he'd scratch, howl, eat the dog's dinner, and – turn into

A Rampaging WEREWO

F!

A NOTE FROM THE AUTHOR

You're probably hoping that I'm now going to tell you exactly what it is that a rampaging Werewolf does. BUT I'M NOT. Because what rampaging werewolves do is... *UNSPEAKABLY HORRID!

(* Which means I can't speak about it, can I – because if I did – it wouldn't be *)

But I'd like to give you some idea. So try imagining this. Imagine a fairly average group of people. For example : –

Three schoolgirls, a baker, two vicars, a ballet dancer, Long John Silver, Napoleon, three Blackburn Rovers supporters, the devil, two musketeers, two ladies-in-waiting, The Queen, Hamlet – Prince of Denmark, and a nephew of Joan of Arc.

Now imagine that early one morning these people were all on a nature ramble in the Derbyshire Peak District. And suddenly, through the swirling mist and rain, they came across the remains of what a RAMPAGING WEREWOLF had done the night before...

THIS IS WHAT THEY MIGHT SAY ➤

NB: If asked to comment further, they would probably say – ( ).*

Now back to the story.

* This is what people often say if asked to describe something which is <u>unspeakable</u>.

Primrose and Cuddles spent a lovely
weekend looking forward to the trip.
So Monday morning came as a shock – for
Miss Fitt was back to her miserable old self.
She read Primrose's list and declared it to
be, **'Sentimental twiddle-twaddle!'**
After reading Cynthia's list she exclaimed,
'Pray God this girl doesn't breed!'
And when she read what Brenda
had written, she screeched –

'How many times must I tell you,

After a while she calmed down.
And – (by means of a cunning combination
of drawn picture and printed text)
she introduced the next Chapter

In which you will learn that werewolves do not exist

Miss Fitt then turned to face the class. 'Werewolves,' she said, 'like unicorns, vampires and fire-breathing dragons, **are *not* real.** They are merely monsters of the imagination.'

Then she said —

I have to go to the office to make further arrangements* for the trip. Take out your 'Webberly-Ward', turn to page 42 and read the chapter entitled 'Myths and legends.' I will ask you some questions when I return.

* She hoped it wasn't too late to <u>cancel it</u>! **

** It was.

boar, hyena, and even cat are were-animals in areas where wolves are not found.

Similar creatures exist in folklore worldwide: for example the tiger,

It is important to remember that these are all myths; stories based upon fear, superstition and wishful thinking. Stories believed by people so simple and primitive that they also believed for instance...

(1) That the Earth was a flat disc balanced on the back of an enormous elephant.

(2) That an erupting volcano was a signal that the Gods were angry.

(3) That by casting a few burnt sticks into a trough of cow dung and noticing the pattern they made, it was possible to foretell the future.

And, who were so naively optimistic as to believe (because it had been foretold by the dung-sticks) that the world was shortly to be taken over by benevolent Martians wearing anoraks, and that one day in the distant future Stoke City would win the FA Cup.

When Miss Fitt returned she said, 'Right. First question: What is "A Myth"?'

Unlucky for some.

CHAPTER THIRTEEN
The day of the trip

I'm not going to write anything about the bus journey to the Derbyshire Peaks.

Why not?

Because nothing of much interest happened.

Fair enough. What about the nature ramble?

Pretty much as you'd expect. Sufficient to say that...

They discovered a pond.

Melanie Penge fell in it.

And Brenda Pigg said –

Ner Nerr Ne-ner-nerr.

Primrose found a beautiful flower.

Oh how sweet. Just look!

Miss Fitt said –

It's a WEED.

And Brenda Pigg stamped on it.

Then Cynthia spotted a flock of *absolutely enormous black-and-white sheep!*
Brenda Pigg started sniggering, and Miss Fitt said, 'Stupid girl! That's a herd of cows!'

And that was about it really.

Nothing 'hideous' or 'unbelievably awful' happened then?

No. Not until four o'clock anyway.

Why? What happened then!?

The bus didn't turn up.

When the bus still hadn't turned up at half-past four the girls began to get worried.
Primrose said –

But Miss Fitt didn't answer.
'I remember seeing a farm back down the road,' said Melanie. 'We could ask the farmer if we could use his phone. My dad could come and get us in the Range Rover.'
Primrose was hesitant. 'Melanie, are you sure you can remember the way to this farm? We don't want to get lost.'
'We'll get lost anyway,' said Brenda Pigg.

'No. It'll be all right. We'll be able to see,' said Cynthia.

'Well then, I vote we give it a try,'
                    said Primrose.
'Can't think of a better idea,'
                    said Cynthia.
'As long as we can get there before dark,'
                    said Brenda.
'What do you think, Miss Fitt?'
                    said Melanie.

But Miss Fitt didn't reply, the reason being
. . . **she wasn't there any more!**

It was from this point on, that some **really interesting things** started to happen.

45

On their way to the farm the girls worked
out what they were going to say.
Cynthia would say —

Then Primrose would say —

We're sorry to bother you
at this late hour, but you
see our bus hasn't arrived.

And then Melanie would say —

Would you let us use
your telephone please?

They were a little concerned that Brenda might then say, **'Or would you like a thick ear!?'**
But in the event, when the farmhouse door opened they said none of these things. Instead they said –

To which Everard Slogg replied

If you were to read the School Prospectus you would learn that –

> At Snobberly House girls are taught
> to understand and speak
> A number of Modern Languages

Unfortunately, Modern Werewolf wasn't one of them.

Which is a pity really, otherwise the girls would have understood that what Everard had just said was –

'Oh how nice – visitors. I was just on my way to the barn, actually. Want to come?'

QUICK! To the BARN!

shouted Primrose.

49

Inside the barn it was pitch black dark.

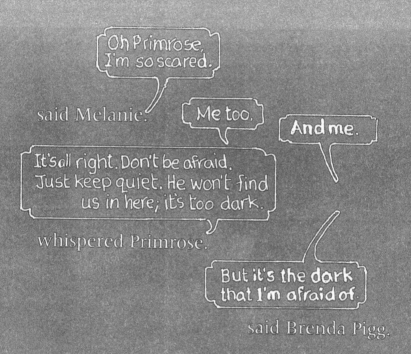

said Melanie.

whispered Primrose.

said Brenda Pigg.

Primrose was surprised by this admission;
she would never have imagined that
Brenda Pigg was afraid of the dark.
Brenda Pigg, she thought, was the sort of
person who wasn't afraid of anything.

50

But Primrose was even more surprised by
what Brenda Pigg said next.

She said –

> Primrose... D'you think I could.. you
> know, because it might make me feel
> safer if... could I?. I mean would you?
> Primrose, please may I have a cuddle
> of your teddy bear... please?

> Of course you may, Brenda.

said Primrose.
And then she said

> OH NO!

And just at that moment, from the
direction of the yard, there came an
awesome blood-curdling howl followed by
a strange eerie silence.
It was just the sort of awesome howl and
eerie silence that a werewolf makes when
the only visitors it's had in two years have
run off and hidden and left it in a state of
anguished rampaging fury – and when it's
just noticed something small, helpless, and
furry lying on the ground by its feet.

51

CHAPTER FOURTEEN

*In which Primrose realizes that she must
have dropped Cuddles when they ran into
the barn and that he is still out there in
the farmyard, and says 'Oh no' – again*

OH NO!

said Primrose
(again).

SSHHhh!

whispered Cynthia.

Or else that big, hairy
sheepdog will hear you and...

Melanie put a hand on
Cynthia's arm. Then quietly
and very gently she said –

Cynthia. There's something you
should know. That thing outside,
it isn't a sheepdog. It's a werewo...

At which point another, much harsher,
louder, and altogether fiercer voice said

52

It was at this point that the girls first became aware of the fact that they were not alone in the barn.

The Snobberly House School Prospectus states quite clearly that –

> The academic staff are all
> **Highly Qualified Educationalists**

What it omits to mention (on account of it being a hideous secret), is that one of them is also a reluctant werewolf.

DOANT LOOOKAT MEEEE AiEEEE LOOOK HiDDEEYUZ!*

howled Miss Fitt.

> Snobberly House encourages girls to develop
> A spirit of fortitude and self-reliance.

What this means in practice is that they are taught how to cope with the sort of crisis which occurs when your knicker elastic breaks in the middle of a gymnastics display. They are *not* taught what they should do if they find themselves cornered in a barn by a werewolf only to find that there's already *another* werewolf in there with them. Thus, at that moment being somewhat deranged, they simply screamed loudly and ran out into the yard. Miss Fitt, being not a little deranged herself, ran after them.

ANOTHER NOTE FROM THE AUTHOR.

Now, as I've already told you, if one rampaging werewolf bumps into a harmless flock of sheep, what usually happens next is UNSPEAKABLY HORRID! Can you imagine what might happen if one deranged and rampaging werewolf were to bump into another deranged and rampaging werewolf!? Well you don't need to because if you turn over the page you'll find out that what happened next was— Miss Fitt leapt howling out into the yard and

. . . was confronted by the sight of . . .

. . . a werewolf in a flat hat singing
lullabies to a teddy bear.

Feeling a strange shadow fall upon him,
the flat-hatted werewolf looked up, and,
seeing the beastly sight before him, said

Which in werewolfspeak means –

6 By Gum, lass. You've got lovely teeth. 9

To which she replied –

In other words –

6 I like your hair. Do you put Brylcream 9
on it, or are you just sweating a lot?

There was a short pause – followed by a
long, strange, staring silence. And then . . .

. . . something very weird and rather wonderful happened.

It was a clear case of love at second sight.

And that's <u>how</u> it was that a small cuddly teddy saved four schoolgirls from being unspeakably rampaged by two werewolves.

And that's <u>why</u> it was that Miss Jennifer Fitt gave up being a lonely schoolmistress – and part-time werewolf – to become instead, a very contented farmer's wife.

And it was also <u>what</u> it was, that made Primrose stop being scared of Brenda Pigg and become instead her very best friend.

And, as far as this story goes, it is also

THE END

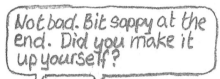

Well. What d'you think?

Not bad. Bit soppy at the end. Did you make it up yourself?

I made the story up, yes. But the <u>underlying</u> <u>message</u> - that's absolutely true. Least <u>I</u> think it is.

The underlying message. What's that?

The story that's between the lines; that you have to work out for yourself. The bit that's supposed to make you <u>think</u>.

Think what?

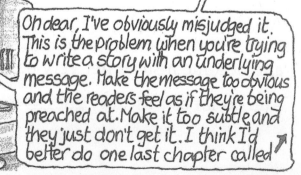

Oh dear, I've obviously misjudged it. This is the problem when you're trying to write a story with an underlying message. Make the message too obvious and the readers feel as if they're being preached at. Make it too subtle and they just don't get it. I think I'd better do one last chapter called ↗

Think about that time when your mum and dad had a big row and your mum stormed out of the house and went to stay with your gran for a few days, and your dad was dead lonely and miserable?
Did you notice a change in his appearance?

Think about the times when your mum gets mad because everybody's arguing at the dinner table. Does she say, 'You lot make me feel like **tearing my hair out?**'
            Does she sometimes screech

At these moments does she look her best?

Remember when your big sister got all depressed about her looks because her boyfriend had finished with her? Did she spend hours in the bathroom putting stuff on her face? If you so much as went near did she shout –

DON'T LOOK at me. I LOOK HIDEOUS*!

* Compare this with page 54.

Have you ever read what it says on that tube of stuff in the bathroom cupboard?

BE WARNED!

And think about this too.
When you are in a mean and miserable mood, and push people about in class, does your teacher tell you how well behaved you used to be; <u>how much you've changed?</u>
Does she sometimes say –

I really dread to think **what** <u>you'll turn into</u> if you carry on like this!!

BE ON YOUR GUARD!

And remember this . . .

. . . often when people are irritable, mean, bad-tempered, and unspeakably horrid to everybody around them, it's not because they <u>want</u> to be.

Sometimes it's just because they feel lost, lonely and unloved.

And, even though it may be that it's <u>you</u> that they're not being very nice to at that moment, **you wouldn't want *them* to turn into a werewolf, would you!?**

So next time you hear your mum or dad complaining of weariness, or notice your brother or sister, one of your friends, or even one of your enemies acting 'were-ish', or looking a bit 'were-ful', you know what to do now – don't you?

Give them A CUDDLE?

CORRECT!